UNTAMED

Created by Dylan Bellis

Written by C. F. Bellis

Acknowledgement

Special thanks to WowWee Untamed® for their creations.

Dedication

This is dedicated to all young dinosaur lovers everywhere.

Four untamed raptors learned to survive in the jungle by using each of their special abilities to help each other.

Their names are Delta, Charlie, Echo, and Blue.

Let's see what their special abilities are.

The first untamed raptor is Delta. He is green, and his ability is his eyesight. Delta could see very far away.

Delta

The second one is Charlie. He is a purple raptor and his special ability is his sharp chomping teeth.

Charlie

The third raptor is Echo. Echo is orange and his special ability is how fast he could run. He was first in every race.

Echo

The fourth and last untamed raptor is Blue, and he is blue. He
is the smartest and fiercest of them all.

Blue

The four raptors were hungry and looking for meat. They are carnivores, meat eaters. Delta saw the meat first because of his great eyesight.

Chomping Charlie and smart, fierce Blue were so hungry, they began to fight over the meat they found.

Finally, fast running Echo got his meat and he kept it all to himself.

Now that the four untamed raptors got their bellies full, they had to find somewhere to sleep for the night.

They searched the jungle for a safe, comfortable place and soon Delta, Charlie, Echo, and Blue found the perfect spot.

They went to sleep hoping for sweet dreams and looking forward to tomorrow's adventures.

The End

Use this page to draw your own dinosaur.

Made in the USA
Middletown, DE
04 September 2023